The Little Red Tortoise

by Amelia Marshall and Evelline Andrya

FRANKLIN WATTS
LONDON • SYDNEY

Long ago, a mother tortoise laid an egg.
One day the egg-shell cracked and out came
a baby tortoise.

The baby tortoise was little
and he was red. So his mother
called him Little Red Tortoise.

It was very hot. It had not rained

for a long time. The field was dusty and dry

and there was no grass to eat.

"I am hungry. Can we go and look for food?"

Little Red Tortoise said to his mother.

"We cannot," said his mother.

"A big, old giraffe lives nearby.

He is very hungry and he likes to eat

little tortoises. If he finds you, he will

swallow you down in one gulp."

Little Red Tortoise did not think that the giraffe

would eat him. He had a clever plan.

"I'll go and get some food for us,"

he said to his mother. And off he went.

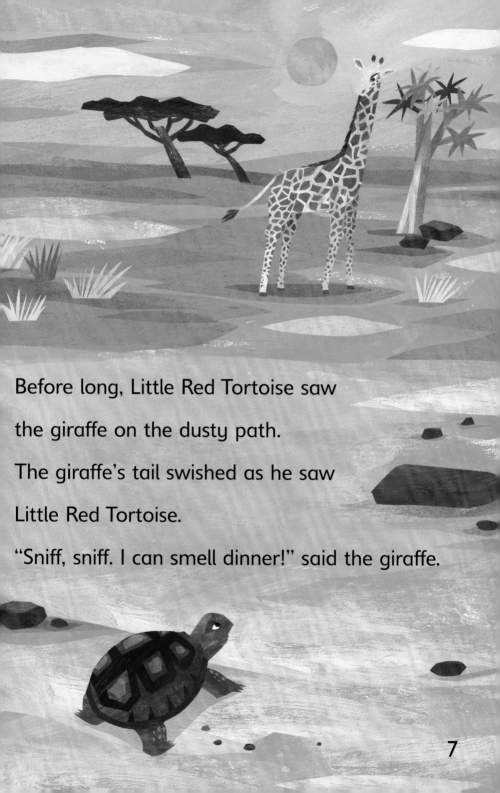

Before long, Little Red Tortoise saw

the giraffe on the dusty path.

The giraffe's tail swished as he saw

Little Red Tortoise.

"Sniff, sniff. I can smell dinner!" said the giraffe.

Little Red Tortoise hid in his shell.

"Come out, come out, Little Red Tortoise,"

said the giraffe. "You can't hide from me."

But Little Red Tortoise didn't move.

He waited .... and waited ... and waited.

The giraffe got more and more angry.

He didn't like to wait.

"Come out," said the giraffe, "or I will squash you with my long legs."

"Ha," said Little Red Tortoise. "Squashing me is much too easy for a big giraffe like you. You need to find another way to eat me."

The giraffe thought about what to do.

"I can swallow bigger animals than you,"

He said. "You are so little.

I can swallow you down in one gulp."

"I don't believe you," said Little Red Tortoise.

"Your throat is too thin. You can not

swallow me."

The giraffe laughed. "Oh yes, I can," he said.

The giraffe bent down his long neck, opened his mouth and swallowed Little Red Tortoise.

But Little Red Tortoise made himself as wide as he could and held on to the side of the giraffe's throat.

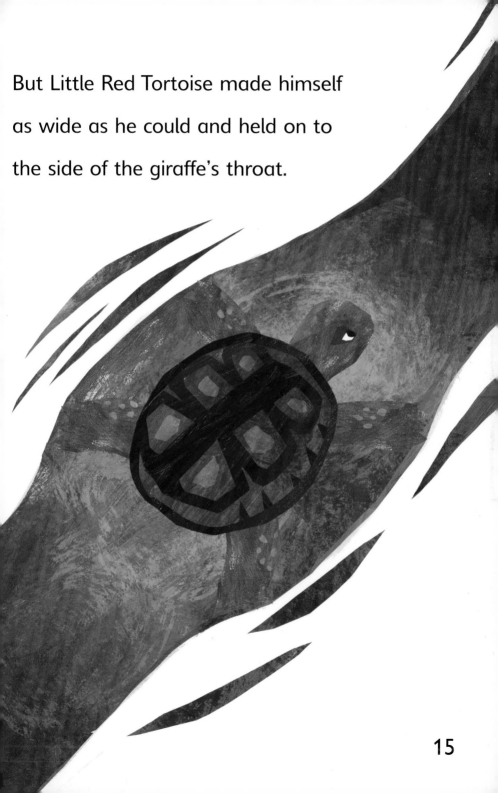

"Stop it, stop it," said the giraffe.

"Go down, go down Little Red Tortoise.

You are choking me," he cried.

But Little Red Tortoise clung on.

"No I won't," he shouted from inside

the giraffe's throat.

"Come up, come up Little Red Tortoise,"

cried the giraffe. "You are choking me."

The giraffe swung and shook this way and that,

but Little Red Tortoise did not move.

The giraffe could not breathe.

He tumbled over onto the sand.

With a gasp, the giraffe sank down into
the sand and opened his mouth.
Little Red Tortoise pushed himself
out of the giraffe's throat.
His plan had worked.

Little Red Tortoise grabbed a big mouthful of

grass and went back to his mother.

"We don't need to be afraid anymore," he said.

"The old giraffe has been beaten."

"Well done, brave Little Red Tortoise!"

said his mother. Little Red Tortoise and his

mother had plenty to eat and the old giraffe

was never seen again.

Story order

Look at these 5 pictures and captions.
Put the pictures in the right order
to retell the story.

1

Giraffe wants to squash Little Red Tortoise.

2

Giraffe starts to choke.

Little Red Tortoise has some grass.

There is not enough food to eat.

Giraffe tries to swallow Little Red Tortoise.

Independent Reading

This series is designed to provide an opportunity for your child to read on their own. These notes are written for you to help your child choose a book and to read it independently.

In school, your child's teacher will often be using reading books which have been banded to support the process of learning to read. Use the book band colour your child is reading in school to help you make a good choice. *Little Red Tortoise* is a good choice for children reading at Gold Band in their classroom to read independently.

The aim of independent reading is to read this book with ease, so that your child enjoys the story and relates it to their own experiences.

About the book

In this world tale from South Africa, Little Red Tortoise is small but brave. When there is no food left to eat, Little Red Tortoise decides to challenge the huge old giraffe who stands in the way. With a clever plan, Little Red Tortoise manages to win and find some fresh grass.

Before reading

Help your child to learn how to make good choices by asking: "Why did you choose this book? Why do you think you will enjoy it?" Look at the cover together and ask: "What do you think the story will be about?" Ask your child to think of what they already know about tortoises in relation to size. Then ask your child to read the title aloud. Ask: "Who else can you see with the Little Red Tortoise?" Remind your child that they can sound out the letters to make a word if they get stuck.

Decide together whether your child will read the story independently or read it aloud to you.

During reading

Remind your child of what they know and what they can do independently. If reading aloud, support your child if they hesitate or ask for help by telling the word. If reading to themselves, remind your child that they can come and ask for your help if stuck.

After reading

Support comprehension by asking your child to tell you about the story. Use the story order puzzle to encourage your child to retell the story in the right sequence, in their own words. The correct sequence can be found on the next page.

Help your child think about the messages in the book that go beyond the story and ask: "Why do you think the Little Red Tortoise challenged the giraffe? Could the giraffe have behaved differently?" Give your child a chance to respond to the story: "Have you ever had to face a difficult situation or overcome a challange? How did you find a resolution? Did you have a plan or did anyone help?"

Extending learning

Help your child predict other possible outcomes of the story by asking: "If it were a different animal living nearby, what do you think might have happened? What animal could it be?" If it had a wider throat, would Little Red Tortoise avoid being eaten?"

In the classroom, your child's teacher may be teaching different kinds of sentences. There are many examples in this book that you could look at with your child, including statements, exclamations and questions. Find these together and point out how the end punctuation can help us decide what kind of sentence it is.

Franklin Watts
First published in Great Britain in 2022
by Hodder and Stoughton

Series Editors: Jackie Hamley and Melanie Palmer
Development Editors and Series Advisors: Dr Sue Bodman and Glen Franklin
Series Designers: Peter Scoulding and Cathryn Gilbert

A CIP catalogue record for this book is
available from the British Library.

ISBN 978 1 4451 8427 2 (hbk)
ISBN 978 1 4451 8428 9 (pbk)
ISBN 978 1 4451 8508 8 (ebook)
ISBN 978 1 4451 8509 5 (library ebook)

Printed in China

Franklin Watts
An imprint of
Hachette Children's Group
Part of Hodder and Stoughton
Carmelite House
50 Victoria Embankment
London EC4Y 0DZ

An Hachette UK Company
www.hachette.co.uk

www.reading-champion.co.uk

Answer to Story order: 4, 1, 5, 2, 3